TIGER'S NEW COWBOY BOOTS

For Virginia,
May your own
boots carry
you far, towards
your most treasured
dreams!
Irene Morck

Georgia Graham

IRENE MORCK   ILLUSTRATIONS BY GEORGIA GRAHAM

Red Deer College Press

Tyler finally had real cowboy boots.

Other years on the cattle drive he'd had to wear running shoes. Nobody wore runners on a cattle drive. Nobody but Tyler, the city kid.

"Woo-ee!" said the salesman. "The cowpokes are gonna be jealous of your boots."

Especially Jessica, thought Tyler. None of her cowboy boots ever looked this good.

It was a long bus ride to Uncle Roy's ranch. But Tyler's boots felt as soft as a pony's nose. He drifted asleep with the sweet smell of new leather.

At sunrise, the lady sitting beside him said, "Oh my, what nice cowboy boots."

"I have to help herd cattle to their summer pasture today," said Tyler. He could hardly stop smiling.

The lady took out a thermos of coffee. The bus hit a bump. Oh no!

"My boots!" cried Tyler.

"Hi, little Tiger," said the cowboy who picked him up at the bus station. "Good thing you came to help. Only six of us riding on this year's drive."

He never noticed Tyler's new boots. Maybe it was too early in the morning. Or maybe there was too much stuff in the truck.

"Four hundred cows and calves," said the cowboy when they stopped above Misty Valley Ranch. "Sure hope we can make them swim the river."

Tyler nodded. He bent to wipe the dust off his boots. The cowboy still didn't notice.

Everyone was waiting. Jessica, Tyler's cousin, had a horse already saddled for him.

"Let's get these cattle moving," said Uncle Roy. "It's going to be a long hot twelve miles to the river."

Cows bellowed to their calves. Calves bawled back. People hollered.

"Hey, Jessica," said Tyler, "did you see my . . ."

But she was already riding away. "Ee-YAAAW! Ee-YAAAW! Ee-YAAAW!"

At the first steep hill the cattle stopped. They didn't want to climb. The riders and horses had to work hard. The cattle started scrambling up the hill—most of them.

A calf darted from the herd. "Get her, Tiger!" yelled one of the cowboys.

Tyler lunged his horse and turned the calf back.

"Poor little critter," said Jessica. "She doesn't care about staying with the rest of the herd. Her mother died last week."

Some cattle tried veering off the trail to hide from the cowboys or the burning sun. Riders chased them back. The forest was deep. You could get lost in no time. "Ee-YAAAW! Ee-YAAAW! Ee-YAAAW!"

Tyler wiped the sweat from his dusty face. When he looked up, the orphan calf was gone.

Branches brushed against Tyler's head, whacked him in the face. He felt scared. Finally Tyler found the calf panting under a bush.

"Get up!" he shouted.

The calf didn't move.

"I'm sorry about your mother," said Tyler, "but we've gotta find the trail again."

The animal just stared.

"Everybody's left us!" Tyler yelled.

Angry now, he jumped off his horse to crawl into the bush after her. With all his strength, he shoved the calf through the tangled branches.

He tripped over a branch, cutting a deep jagged scratch across his boot. But there wasn't time to even think about that now.

The cattle drive wore on. The smallest calves shuffled farther and farther behind. Tyler felt dizzy from hunger and heat.

They reached a clearing. At last everyone could rest. The cattle lay down, too tired to moo.

Time for lunch.

Mustard squirted from Tyler's sandwich. He jumped back and stepped in something worse. Yuck!

Would Jessica—or anybody—see these boots before they were completely wrecked?

"Maybe this heat will make the cattle want to swim," said a cowboy.

"It's swim or a mighty long truck ride," said Uncle Roy. The nearest bridge was sixty miles away. Bounced for hours over gravel roads last year, eight calves got sick with shipping fever.

And you could buy a hundred pair of cowboy boots for what Uncle Roy would have to pay to truck the cattle.

After their rest, the herd moved on again. About two o'clock they reached a creek. The animals strode into the cool water. This creek wasn't deep or wide like the big river—the river that had drowned a calf one year.

Tyler lifted his feet so the creek water couldn't splash his boots. Wet leather would dry all stiff and dull.

"Hey, Tyler. Watch out!" Jessica was shouting. "Your friend is escaping again."

"Some friend," said Tyler, heading after the orphan calf. "Call her Trouble."

"There's the river!" said Jessica. "Wow, it's higher than normal. Must have been raining a lot up in the mountains."

The river looked real scary. But first they had to chase all four hundred cattle into the huge holding corral on the riverbank.

When the cows and calves were trapped, ready for the crossing, Uncle Roy barked out orders to get everyone in place.

"Tyler," he said, "you stand your horse in the water—right beside that panel. Don't let any cattle escape around it."

A cowboy opened the gate for three cows to lead the way. Riders, hollering, chased them toward the water.

The first cow plunged in, surfaced and started swimming. Everybody whooped and cheered. The second cow hit the water.

Tyler didn't realize the current was pulling his horse downstream. The third cow noticed a space widening between the panel and Tyler's horse. The cow slipped past and charged up the bank.

Tyler raced after her. In the confusion, the first two cows turned and swam back. They got away, too.

By the time those three cows were rounded up, it was after five o'clock. Tyler couldn't bear to look at anyone. He'd let them down.

When the crossing started again, he kept his horse tight against the panel.

"No getting by me this time," he muttered to himself.

Suddenly the cattle were swimming! Calves disappeared under the water, then bobbed up, wide-eyed, snorting and struggling. Somehow each one figured out how to swim.

Needing every bit of energy, cows and calves swam silently. On the other bank, the cattle scrambled up, dripping wet, bawling again.

Tyler forced the few remaining calves toward the water. At last they jumped in. All except one. Little Trouble.

Yelling, he crowded his horse against the trembling calf, but she was too scared to jump in.

Tyler leaped off his horse. He sloshed through the water and mud. Before the startled riders could say a thing, he was shoving Trouble down the bank, her tiny hooves skidding every which way.

His muscles ached, but Tyler kept pushing and heaving until that calf tumbled—splash!—into the river.

"Way to go, Tiger!" shouted Uncle Roy. Jessica grinned.

Tyler vaulted onto his horse to follow Trouble. Ice-cold water flooded his boots.

He kept his horse swimming right beside the calf, terrified each time her face disappeared under the water, thrilled each time it reappeared.

"Ee-YAAAW! Ee-YAAAW! Ee-YAAAW!" he hollered. "We're almost there!"

Beyond the river, time disappeared in a blur. Tyler's wet jeans started to dry. The water in his boots warmed up and felt good sloshing between his toes.

Finally the herd reached their summer meadow.

Tyler collapsed in the grass, almost too tired to speak.

"Wow—check it out," said one of the cowboys. "Tiger's got real cowboy boots."

Tyler looked at his muddy, stained, soggy, cut-up boots. "They're real all right," he said, half-smiling. "Maybe . . . too real."

Jessica trudged over to Tyler and flopped down beside him.

"Hey, Tiger," she said, "your boots are just like mine."

Northern Lights Books for Children are published by
Red Deer College Press
56 Avenue & 32 Street Box 5005
Red Deer Alberta Canada T4N 5H5

Acknowledgments
Edited for the Press by Tim Wynne-Jones
Cover and text design by Kunz + Associates
Printed in Hong Kong by Artfield Printing for Red Deer College
Press

5 4 3 2 1

Financial support provided by the Alberta Foundation for the Arts,
a beneficiary of the Lottery Fund of the Government of Alberta,
and by the Canada Council, the Department of Canadian Heritage
and Red Deer College.

COMMITTED TO THE DEVELOPMENT OF CULTURE AND THE ARTS

Morck, Irene.
Tiger's new cowboy boots
(Northern lights books for children)
ISBN 0-88995-153-5
1. Cattle drives–Alberta–Juvenile fiction. 2. Ranch life–Alberta–
Juvenile fiction. I. Graham, Georgia, 1959– II. Title. III. Series.
PS8576.O628T53 1996   jC813'.54   C96-910307-7
PZ7.M7885Ti 1996

*For two people no longer here—Mogens' mom and my dad. I still feel the sound of their boots walking through every day
with me.*
– Irene Morck

*To my in-laws—Don, Brenda, Jenny and Matt Graham, who are the real cowboys of Misty Valley Ranch. Their beautiful
ranch and unique lifestyle were my inspiration for this book. Thanks especially to Matt, who posed for Tiger.*
– Georgia Graham